DRAMA CLUB

Marie-Louise Jensen

FICTION
EXPRESS

What do other readers think?

Here are some comments left on the Fiction Express blog about this book:

"'Drama Club' is EPIC! I love the characters in it and the actual story!"
Megan Stoves, Staffordshire

"I love the 'Drama Club' book, I'm so desperate for the next chapter."
Holly, York

"'Drama Club' is the best book so far. I love the characters in it."
James, Telford

"NO.1 FAN I LOVE YOUR BOOKS"
Abdullah, Birmingham

"We are reading 'Drama Club' at school and I love it! You are an amazing author."
Lauren, Staffordshire

Contents

*With thanks to my hard-working editor
Laura Durman and all the students who
read and voted on 'Drama Club' when it was
being written as an interactive e-book.*

Chapter 1

New Beginnings

I wait for my friends on the corner of Lime Avenue with a flutter of excitement in my stomach. It's the middle of the day – baking hot – and I'm wishing I hadn't got here early. A wind like a blast from a hairdryer blows down the street, making the litter whirl wildly in the gutter. An empty crisp packet flies up and sticks in someone's dusty hedge: a ragged butterfly caught in a web.

I've been looking forward to today for weeks – the start of our summer drama club, Footlights. I wouldn't like to admit to anyone how excited I am because they might think I'm lame. But for me, Footlights *is* the summer holidays.

Indira is the first to arrive. She strides down the street towards me, her long black hair tumbling over her shoulders. She's taller than me and gorgeous with her creamy brown skin and sparkling dark eyes.

"Hey, Zoe!" she cries as she reaches me.

"Good to see you!" I say, hugging her. "Did you have a nice week away?"

"It was OK," she replies. "I'm glad to be back though."

Luchi lopes up to us grinning. He's dressed in football shorts, a tank top with a loose shirt over it and trainers. As usual, he hasn't bothered with socks or with the laces. I don't know how he manages to make being scruffy look cool, but he always does. "'Sup?" he says by way of hello. "So where's Alfie?" We all look at each other and shrug.

"We'd better fetch him," says Indira.

Alfie's asleep in his garden, stretched out on the grass in chinos and a t-shirt. Luchi sneaks up and crouches behind him, then shouts "Alfie!" right in his ear.

"Wha'?" Alfie sits up hurriedly, rubbing his hand over his face, knocking his glasses crooked.

"Had you forgotten?" demands Indira.

"Absolutely not!" says Alfie groggily. "I'm on it! Was just chilling… soaking up some rays."

"That reminds me, I need to work on *my* tan this summer," says Luchi. He grins as he slips off his shirt and glances down at the rich-chocolate hue of his arms. "I'm way too pale after a year in school."

Alfie laughs. I stare at Luchi's brown arms, wondering when they got so… muscular. Then I look away, too shy to say anything. But Indira says it. Shyness is not a concept she's ever bothered with. "You been working out, Luchi?" she asks.

"Nah. This is all natural, innit!" says Luchi, sauntering towards us.

Alfie follows behind, still as skinny as ever. "So where are we going?" he asks.

We all groan. "Footlights!" Indira tells him.

"Course." Jumping over the low fence, Alfie joins us on the pavement. "What are we waiting for?" he asks.

* * *

"Welcome everyone!" says Badger looking around at us as we sit on the floor in the small theatre. He's a tall, wiry man with bright blue eyes and boundless enthusiasm. His name is Mr Beaven, really, but he has a strange grey streak in his hair so, behind his back, we call him Badger. We don't mean anything by it, though. Without him, there would be no drama club. He's the best.

"It's great to see such a crowd of you here today. Lots of familiar faces and some new ones, too." Badger rubs his hands together. "Excellent!"

I look at the new members. There's a tall girl who catches my eye. She has glimmering, golden hair that reaches right down to her waist. 'Goldie' notices me watching her and screws up her pretty face as if she's caught a whiff of something gross. She turns away and does this flicky thing with her hair.

I glare at the back of her head. She's standing with two other girls. One is Alice, who was bound to take up with a new girl seeing as she's not very popular. She's got a mean way with her at times. But I don't recognize the other girl – she must be new too. Mascara glues her eyelashes together and her blusher is coated on in orange stripes. Not a great look – definitely no match for Goldie.

There are two new boys, and a girl in a wheelchair – I wonder how *that* will work out in a drama group. She looks really nice, though, and her hairstyle is cool. She sees me looking at her and we exchange shy smiles. I already prefer her to Goldie.

"I know you're all keen to know what we're going to be working on over the next five weeks," Badger is saying, and my attention snaps back to him instantly. This is what I've been waiting for! At Christmas we did *The Lion, the Witch and the Wardrobe*, which was brilliant.

"And the play I've chosen for us this summer…." says Badger. "Drum roll, please!"

We drum on the floor and then fall silent. Badger grins delightedly at his own joke and pauses dramatically, as if it's *The X-Factor* or something.

I can hear Luchi muttering quietly beside me: "Not Shakespeare, not Shakespeare." I grin nervously at him. I can hardly breathe.

"It's going to be… *Beauty and the Beast*!" Badger says.

There's a gasp of excitement from every girl in the room. I'm pretty sure we're all imagining ourselves as Beauty. At least, that's what I'm doing. I shiver with anticipation.

At the same time, I hear a groan from the boys. "Ugh, not that soppy Disney rubbish," says Luchi looking disappointed.

"Don't worry," says Alfie smirking. "Maybe you'll get to be a dancing teacup!"

"This is NOT the Disney version," says Badger,

overhearing. "This is a teen script and I think you'll all love it – boys too!" He's looking straight at Luchi.

Luchi opens his mouth to reply when a loud voice breaks through the excited buzz of chatter.

"Will there be auditions, sir?" asks Goldie eagerly. She shakes her hair so that it catches the light.

"Not as such," says Badger. "Er…." He glances down at his list of names, trying to place her.

"Lauren," she tells him, flicking her hair again.

"Well, Lauren, we'll warm up with drama games, do some improvisations and role plays, and read through the first scenes. I'll take decisions about who is best for the different roles and announce the cast tomorrow. Are you new to drama, Lauren?"

"I played Annie in the school play last year and I take jazz and tap classes," says Lauren confidently. "Oh, and I've been an extra in *Casualty*."

Badger looks impressed as Lauren nudges Alice. Yep. She's sure she's bagged it already. A bitter taste spreads in my mouth. She'll get the lead. No doubt about it. With all that experience, she must be good! She's certainly pretty and has got legs up to her armpits. How can I compete with that? Ugh.

All at once, it's as though the sun's gone behind a raincloud.

Chapter 2

Fortunately, Unfortunately

I've got a secret that I haven't told anyone, not even Indira. I desperately want to be an actor... maybe even be famous one day. If I'm lucky enough to get a main role this summer, I'd have to attend *all* the rehearsals. It would get me out of the flat... away from mum and her loser 'boyfriend'. Believe me, I need that more than anything. I'm terrified Lauren is going to spoil all that for me.

"Right! Time to get to know each other!" says Badger. The sound of his voice draws my attention back to what's happening around me.

"Sit in a circle!" he says. Whoever catches the ball calls out their name and tells us one interesting thing about themselves."

"I love this game," whispers Alfie.

"It's lame AS, dude!" says Luchi as we all shuffle back.

Lauren and her friends end up next to me. Badger tosses a big squashy ball to me so I can begin.

"I'm Zoe," I call out, "and I love the theatre!" I look

around the circle wondering whose name I'd like to know. I throw it to the girl in the wheelchair.

She looks as if she's going to catch it, but at the last minute her arm jerks and she misses. The ball rolls away and I feel awful. "I'm sorry!" I say. "That was a rubbish throw."

The girl looks annoyed with herself, but shrugs. "That's all right," she replies in a clear voice. "My name's Taylor. I want to be a fashion designer… and, as you can see, I'm rubbish at catching, too." To my relief she smiles at me. I relax as some of the others laugh at Taylor's joke.

Badger gives her back the ball. "Sorry, Taylor," he says. "My mistake choosing a co-ordination game when…."

I don't hear the rest, because Lauren leans over to the girls next to her and whispers. I don't catch what she says, but I'm sure it's about Taylor. They all explode in giggles. I'm shocked. I didn't think anyone here would be so mean. Luchi leans towards them from the other side and glares at them. Did he think they were sniping about Taylor too? We should say something. But the game is moving on so we don't.

Luchi tells us his mum named him after her favourite Jamaican singer – Luciano. Lauren smiles at him and flicks her hair… *again*. She obviously has a crush on him already. But when Alfie says he wants to be an app developer, I hear Lauren whisper "Geek-boy". I was angry before. There must be steam coming off me by now.

"Shut it, Goldilocks!" I hiss.

"Oo-oo-ooh," Lauren mocks, smirking at her new friends.

"I was just saying how nice your jumper is, Zoe. Did you get it in a charity shop?" They all snort with laughter.

"Quiet please, girls," says Badger, eyeballing me even though I'm not remotely the one laughing.

Lauren's other friend (who also drops the ball when it's thrown to her, so that serves *her* right) is called Bailey. She says she wants to be a model. I guess that explains all the make-up.

We split into groups and play ten-second objects. We have ten seconds to use our bodies to make whatever objects Badger calls out. I like my group and we laugh trying to make a peacock and then a car together.

The most exciting bit comes after we've done some role playing. Badger hands out scripts and we sit down to start the read-through. The script's really modern and gets lots of laughs, even from Luchi.

"That was a fabulous start!" says Badger at the end of the afternoon. "You all read brilliantly. Well done! Remember we need to put on a really good show at the end of the summer to impress the council so they'll keep funding us! I'll invite some councillors to the performance as usual. With your help and dedication we'll knock their socks off! So, tomorrow I'll assign the roles and then we'll do some hot seating to start building up a picture of our characters. We'll play one last game today: split into pairs for 'Fortunately Unfortunately'. I'll start you off – Fortunately, we're going to put on the best play ever this summer!"

I pair up with Luchi and we get started while Badger explains the game to the newbies. He's got a pen and clipboard in his hand and has been making notes all afternoon.

"Fortunately, we have some fine actors in this group," says Luchi to me, winking. I grin back. I've known Luchi since forever and I'm comfortable working with him.

"Unfortunately, they're not all as nice as you and me," I say.

"Fortunately, they're not as cool either," says Luchi. I choke.

"Unfortunately, they're being mean about our friends," I point out.

"Fortunately, we won't let them spoil anyone's fun."

"Unfortunately, one of them is so stunning, she will probably get to play Beauty," I say. Oops. That wasn't meant to come out as bitter as it did.

"Fortunately, Badger isn't stupid," says Luchi.

"What was that about badgers?" asks Mr Beaven appearing behind Luchi, clipboard poised. We both crack up.

* * *

"This summer's going to be brilliant!" exclaims Indira, as we walk home along the dusty streets of the estate. Most of the houses used to have front gardens, but now they have cars parked on them instead. "Badger's chosen a great play."

"Definitely," says Alfie, kicking an empty can along. The rattle echoes between the houses. "I hope I'll get to do the sound and lighting this time. I already have some great ideas for the beast scenes."

"Why would you want to be stuck in a pokey sound room?" asks Indira. "You could *be* the beast instead!"

"Nah!" Alfie grins and kicks the can away. It clatters along the gutter.

"You just love those banks of little switches and flashing lights, don't you, mate?" says Luchi, slinging a brotherly arm around his friend's shoulders. Alfie shrugs him off good-naturedly.

"So what do we make of the new kids?" Indira asks.

"We do not like Miss Goldilocks," I say emphatically.

"Too right," Luchi agrees.

"Lauren? Is she that bad?" asks Indira, who wasn't sitting near her.

"YES," Luchi and I chorus.

"She was having a go at Taylor," I add.

"That's well out of order," growls Indira. "I paired up with Taylor. She's cool."

"Yeah, well, I was partnered with Lauren and she's a brilliant actor!" Alfie pipes up.

"What?" I shout, louder than I meant to. How did I not notice Alfie teaming up with Goldie?

"Yeh, and she's pretty, too," he continues. "I think she should get the part of Beauty."

Indira and I stop in our tracks. "You'd rather she played Beauty than *me*… or *Indira*?"

"That's not what he said, Zo'," interrupts Luchi.

"Yeah, I didn't mean it like that," Alfie spluttered, realizing he's upset me. "I'm just saying she's got loads of experience. And that's important for the lead role, isn't it? We all want the play to be great, don't we? For the funding and everything!"

Deep down I know that Alfie is right. I *should* want what's best for everyone not just me. But I really don't want Lauren to get that part.

"Her parents must be loaded." I mutter. "You can tell just by looking at her. Why isn't she hanging out at Stagecoach with all the other rich kids?"

There's a Stagecoach theatre school not far from our estate, but it costs hundreds of pounds to go there. Footlights is free – the council funds it for kids with no money. Kids like us. It's *our* group.

"Her dad lost his job this spring," says Alfie. "That's why she's had to give up Stagecoach and join our group. I feel sorry for her. It can't be easy moving like that."

"Dude, how much time did you spend with her?" asks Luchi.

As we make our way home, Alfie peels off and heads up his road. Some of the houses are empty and the windows have been boarded up. Colourful graffiti decorates the wooden panels.

The rest of us live in the flats further along. The blocks rise out of the ground like concrete monsters. The council recently gave them a 'facelift' – new blue balconies and white windows. From this distance, they still look as grey and soulless as ever, though.

"This'll be a great play, Zoe," says Indira confidently, after we've dropped Luchi off at his place. "I hope *you* get to be Beauty."

I flush with pleasure. "Or you!" I say quickly. "You'd be amazing!"

"Nah, my mum wants me to study, not spend all my time at Footlights rehearsals," says Indira with a sigh. "You know what she's like: Why are you wasting your time acting, Indira?" She waggles her forefinger, doing an impression of her mum. "If you want to be a doctor, you must study, study, study!"

"I thought you wanted to act?" I ask, confused. Indira grins mischievously.

"Of course I do! Don't worry, I'll get my way in the end. But I've got to study as well so...." She grimaces. "You know how it is. Parents love to give you grief."

I think of my mum, who's always exhausted and grumpy from looking after the twins, and of her boyfriend, who never gets off my case. "I know *exactly* what you mean," I sigh.

"To tell the truth," Indira confides. "I'd *love* to play Beauty. It'd be awesome."

"Yeah," I agree. "I want to so much it hurts. But if I don't get it, I'd love you to. I could help you learn the lines."

Indira laughs. "Perfect!"

I try to laugh too but I don't quite manage it. "I'm terrified Badger will pick Lauren," I admit. "That would spoil the whole holiday. Imagine what she'll be like if she's the star of the show!"

We both groan. The summer I've been looking forward to for so long has a dark shadow over it. A Lauren-shaped shadow.

Chapter 3

Decisions, Decisions

When we arrive at the theatre the next afternoon, Lauren is already there. She's perched on the edge of the stage next to Mr Beaven and she looks like the cat that got the cream. Not just a little dish either – the entire potful.

"*Surely* not?" I whisper to Indira. She slips her hand into mine and grips it hard.

"Start saying your prayers," she says gloomily.

"Sit down, folks, and listen," says Badger. I squeeze Indira's hand in anticipation of Badger's decision – hoping I will be Beauty – but his voice is grave. "I'm afraid I have some upsetting news."

I shiver. Something's really wrong. I can see it in his face. For a moment, I forget all about Lauren and sit down between Indira and Alfie, quiet as a mouse. You can feel the tension in the air.

"I'm sorry to tell you, I've had a letter from the council," Badger explains. He looks exhausted – there are lines on his face I've never noticed before. "They've got to make massive cuts to arts funding across the city. That means Footlights will have to close."

At first there's complete silence. And then "Noooooo!" There's an outcry from all of us. "That's not fair!" cries Indira.

I can't speak. I'm stricken with horror.

"It's not fair and it's not right," says Badger. "But I've been expecting something like this for a while. They've already closed the library and the youth club… it was always likely we could be next."

"But we've got this summer, haven't we?" asks Luchi. "And they still might change their mind when they see our show."

"The cuts are effective from three weeks' time," says Badger sadly. "That's a fortnight before the show. We can continue with drama for three weeks, but we won't be able to put on the production. We'll have no way of paying for the hall hire, the costumes, printing tickets…."

There's a cough from the back of the hall. "I'm sorry to hear about this," says Mr Jones – he owns the theatre and plays piano for us, too. "If it's any help, you can forget the rent for the last two weeks. We all want to see your show. We love having you here."

"That's so kind," says Badger. "But I still don't see…."

"I can make the costumes," pipes up Taylor. "It's what I wanted to do anyway. I'm sure everyone's got bits and pieces at home – old clothes we can cut up. Or curtains. And there are the charity shops!"

"Wow, Taylor, thank you, I–"

"We can sell tickets to the show!" says Alfie.

Tears start to well up in Badger's eyes and his voice is all choked. He clears his throat, pulling himself together. "You are all so fantastic," he says. "I'll forego my fee of course. But there will be other things we need, like a dance teach–"

"We could hold a cake sale," Bailey pipes up. "We could all bring a cake and raise money."

Lots of other kids shout out suggestions. "My uncle can print the tickets at work!" calls Indira.

"Please," I add. "Please, Mr Beaven. Don't let them close us down before the show."

Badger looks around at us all, rubs his hand across his forehead and looks a little helplessly at Mr Jones. "Very well," he says at last. "Let's see how we go!"

"Yes!" we all punch the air and cheer. I'm determined to work all summer if I have to, to keep the drama club open. Anything's better than losing it.

"Right then," says Badger, once we're all facing him again. "I guess it's time to announce the roles. Please remember, everyone, *every* part is important in this play! For the role of Beauty, I've chosen…."

My heart starts to pound as some of the boys drum on the floor.

"LAUREN!" Badger cries, grinning.

Lauren smirks. Did she already know? She doesn't seem surprised.

I'm sick with disappointment. I wanted to be Beauty so badly. But now Badger's calling my name out: "Sister 1 is Zoe; Sister 2 is Bailey. The Mother will be played by Indira."

He pauses and looks at his list. "And Beast will be… LUCHI!"

So I'm one of the mean sisters. They are vile to Beauty all the way through. At least I'll get to be nasty to Lauren – that makes me feel a bit better. It wouldn't have been so much fun the other way around, that's for sure!

I hear Badger telling Alfie he will be in charge of sound and lighting. He looks made up about it. Taylor says that she'll be too busy making costumes to learn lines, so she'd prefer to help backstage. Badger asks her whether she could be prompter on the show nights, and she agrees. A boy called Will is going to be Father and the two new boys will play the brothers. Everyone else will be the Beast's servants or will play horses.

Badger puts us straight into groups to do hot seating – to learn more about our characters. Unfortunately, I'm in a group with Lauren and Bailey, because we're the three sisters.

"It's so awesome you're going to be Beauty, Lauren," Bailey gushes. "You'll be *amazing*!"

"Yeah, well," says Lauren looking around the hall disparagingly. "There's no one else in this group of losers who could make a decent job of it. They're lucky I joined."

I gasp and Lauren hears me. She stares at me and grins. "You didn't honestly think that *you* would get to play Beauty, did you, Zo'? Aww, you *did*, didn't you? Oh no, are you going to cry now?" She and Bailey giggle together.

"Get over yourself, Lauren," I say, trying to ignore the

sick feeling in my stomach. "And the name's Zoe, with an 'e'. I only let my friends call me Zo'!"

"OK, OK. Anwyay, look, I'll start the game," says Lauren. "I've got the star role – the most challenging part in the whole play, after all."

She's boasting now and has raised her voice. Luchi, in the next group, overhears and looks round. "No, mine is the most difficult," he says. He leaves a pause and a puzzled frown creases Lauren's pretty forehead. "I mean, *dude*," continues Luchi turning to Alfie but still speaking loudly so Lauren will hear. "I've got to pretend to be ugly! That will take *serious* talent!"

The boys snigger. Lauren smiles, and flicks her hair. "But you'll be my handsome prince at the end!" she says. I swear she actually flutters her eyelashes.

I expect Luchi to come out with some more banter but he doesn't, he *actually* smiles back at her! I glance at Alfie: he looks a bit miffed.

Then Badger comes over, wondering why we haven't started yet, so we get to work. Of course, Lauren *does* go first. Badger stays to listen and when she's done, he says, "What you need to bear in mind above all, Lauren, is that Beauty is good and kind and she *always* thinks of others before herself. You're doing really well, excellent. Carry on! Zoe, your turn."

He walks off and I turn to Lauren. "I think Luchi was wrong, you know," I say. "You really *have* got the hardest part."

Lauren looks pleased. "Told you so," she says, totally not expecting me to be nasty.

"Yeah, really, because you're going to have a tough time pretending to be *nice!*"

Lauren gives me the evils. "Well, I can see you're not going to need acting skills for *your* role."

You have to hand it to her, Lauren's got a quick answer for everything.

"Just getting in training," I say with a grin.

Chapter 4

Dance Drama

"Make sure you all begin a 'role on the wall' at home tonight!" calls Badger as we leave.

"What's a 'role on the wall'?" Taylor asks me on the way out.

"Oh, that's where you draw your character on a big sheet of paper," I explain, "And write down things about them. Like what things they like or hate or what they're good at."

"Oh, I don't need to worry about that, then," says Taylor with a smile. "I'll start designing costumes instead."

"Can you really do that?" I ask, awed. "I can't even sew on a button."

"Yes, I can. I love it."

"We need to have a meeting," says Indira, marching up and interrupting. "We need to get a campaign going, Zoe. Are you with us?"

"A campaign?" I ask, bewildered.

"Yes, to save Footlights! It's all very well we're safe

for this summer. But we need to persuade the council to change their minds so we can carry on at Christmas – and every other holiday, too! They can't just close us down! Me, you, Alfie and Luchi and anyone else who wants to help."

"Yes, of course I'm with you," I say eagerly.

"Cool! Where shall we go to talk? Can we go to yours?"

"Oh, I er… not really," I say, imagining what mum's boyfriend would say if we all walked in.

"Nor mine," says Luchi. "My mum's on nights. She'll be asleep."

"Nah, my house is a tip," says Alfie.

"Come to mine," says Taylor unexpectedly. "I live just around the corner. If you want to…."

"Brilliant!" says Indira at once. "Of course – you're one of us, Taylor! Let's go!"

* * *

Taylor's house is a small bungalow that has been adapted for her wheelchair. Her mum is lovely and gets us all squash and biscuits.

"Plan of campaign," says Indira, getting out a notebook and a pencil. She is so organized it's ridiculous. Where would we be without her? "Number One: A petition."

"Number Two: A demonstration," says Taylor. We all stare. "That's what we did when they cut our disability benefits," she explains. "We got banners and stuff and chained our wheelchairs to the railings outside the Houses of Parliament."

"*You* did that?" I ask, awed.

"Yep."

"Cool!" says Luchi. "Did it make a difference?"

"No… but that was the government. This is the city council, right here where we live. It's worth a try."

"Right," agrees Alfie. "Sounds good. What else?"

We write down a list of ideas and agree to think them over before the next day. We enlist Taylor's mum to bake something for our cake sale and we all head home.

A peace has fallen over our estate, as it always does at this time of day. The roar of traffic from the main road has faded to a whisper.

Loud voices shatter the quietness as we turn a corner. A group of teens is larking about and climbing in one of the newly-planted trees at the side of the road. It's not strong enough and a whole branch snaps off. The kids run away, laughing guiltily.

Indira looks sadly at the torn branch, the trampled soil and the scattered litter and sighs. "Good job we've got something better to do this summer than *that*," she remarks. "We *have* to get the council to see sense. They've got to give us something to do all day."

"You could study," I remind her.

"Oh great, thanks!" The sarcasm drips off Indira's voice.

* * *

I get to Footlights early the next day as I have some stuff to do in town beforehand. Lauren is already there and she's on the stage, dancing. Badger is sitting on a chair watching – he doesn't even notice me walk in. And next to him, completely mesmerised, is Alfie. *Alfie*! The traitor!

I don't want to look, but my eyes are drawn to the stage. I'm completely stunned. Where did she learn to dance like that? It's *amazing*.

"That is fabulous, Lauren," says Badger as she finishes. "I can see you're absolutely right and we won't need to hire a dance teacher after all, which makes the finances for this summer much easier."

He turns to me. "Oh, hello Zoe, nice to see you. Lauren's choreographed this dance for the show. What do you think?"

"It's… it's incredible," I say. I so don't want to flatter Lauren's ego, but it's the truth.

"She's going to teach you all the routine, starting this afternoon," says Badger.

"Can't wait," I say, the enthusiasm gone from my voice. Lauren notices, but Badger doesn't.

"I'm sure you're a star dancer, Zoe," says Lauren under her breath. "Which dance school did you say you went to? Oh… wait…."

I don't answer because she's right. I've never been able to afford dance lessons. I only know the bits and pieces I've picked up here at Footlights over the last couple of years. But I'm an actor, not a dancer.

Badger is talking again: "This playscript asks for a lot of dancing. We had two options really. To adapt it to leave it out, or to get a dance teacher in, which we no longer have funding for. But now, thanks to Lauren…."

I tune him out. He's right of course, it's great. But it's *Lauren*. Why does she have to be so good at everything?

I sit down with Alfie as the others start arriving. He can't take his eyes off Lauren who's stretching out, practising her steps. "Hey Alfie," I say, clicking my fingers. "Would you like me to write '*I am dead impressed*' on your forehead?"

"Sorry, Zo'," says Alfie, blushing.

The dancing goes better than I expected. Lauren hasn't got time to be nasty when she's teaching us, and she wouldn't want to show herself up in front of Badger anyway. I really enjoy learning the routine and find it easier than I expect.

"You're a natural, Zoe," says Luchi afterwards.

"And you," I tell him. "You're brilliant!" Luchi shrugs it off but I can tell he's pleased. "How come Indira didn't show today?"

"I'm not sure," I reply. "I texted her earlier but didn't hear back. Hope she's ok."

We begin rehearsing our lines in the last hour and learning where we'll be standing on stage during each scene. It's all starting to seem real. I get that feeling I always get when I'm acting. A sort of flying feeling. Energy buzzes through me.

At the end, Alice sidles up to me. "Zoe," she says. "I designed a leaflet for the cake sale. Do you want to see it?"

"Sure," I say, surprised.

She fishes it out of her bag and it's really good. She's drawn some cartoons and fancy lettering on it. "This is awesome!" I tell her. "I didn't know you were into art."

Alice goes pink. "I just need the dates," she says. "Then perhaps Indira can get a load printed."

I need to get everyone's attention. I really wish Indira was here – she's good at that. She'd stand on a chair and shout. I give it a go, but no one listens until Badger sees me. "Quiet everyone," he says. "Zoe wants to say something."

"We need to decide a date for the cake sale!" I say nervously. "Can we hold it here, during a rehearsal? Would that be all right, Mr Jones?"

"As long as I get some free cake," says the theatre owner with a grin.

"How about a week on Friday?" says Badger.

"Actually, a weekend would be better," says Mr Jones. "You would get more customers. The theatre is free a week on Saturday in the morning. You can use the kitchen as long as you clean up after yourselves."

"Brilliant, thank you!" replies Badger. "That's agreed then."

"Everyone needs to bring a cake!" says Taylor. "And to help with the sales. Should we do teas and coffees too?"

"Definitely!" I say. "I'll help."

"I'll do the leaflet drop," says Luchi. "You'll help me, won't you, Alfie?"

Alfie nods.

* * *

I check my phone as we're leaving. Indira has finally texted:

Had 2 stay home 2 babysit sis :-(Call 4 me 2moz? Xx

"That's harsh," says Luchi when I tell the others.

"Yeh, and she's got a lot to catch up on," says Alfie. We're walking home together and tonight it's less hot; there's a breeze freshening the air.

"I'll come with you to call for her tomorrow," Luchi says. "Make sure she comes!"

"I'm sure she won't skip another rehearsal," I say. "Think of all the gossip she's missed out on!"

* * *

When we get to Indira's the following afternoon, Luchi doesn't knock on the door, because her parents aren't always that friendly to us. We go around the back and throw pebbles at Indira's window instead. It's lucky she's on the ground floor.

The window opens straight away, and Indira looks out.

"Hey hun, you missed loads of choreography yesterday!" I say. "But don't worry – you'll pick it up really quickly after all your classical Indian dance training!"

"Don't. Just don't," snaps Indira and I suddenly see she's been crying. "It's all over for me. Mum and Dad say I've got to *study*. They even took away my mobile!"

"But it's, like, the summer holidays!" says Luchi. "Man, that's rough!"

"But…." I say. "You mean just today, right… or this week?"

"It's ALL SUMMER!!! No more Footlights for me!" Indira sounds as if she's about to start crying again.

"You can't be serious!" I say. "There's the campaign and everything! We need you!"

"Not as badly as I need you and Footlights!" says Indira with a groan. "Look, I'm working on my parents, OK? I'm doing my best! Maybe if I study hard this week they'll ease up a bit."

"I hate leaving you like this," I say sadly.

"We'll be back," Luchi promises.

"Text me when you can," I say, but Indira just sighs.

Chapter 5

Causes and Consequences

It's Monday afternoon and Luchi and I are tapping on Indira's window again. It opens and we're relieved to see her peep out.

"'Sup, Indira?" asks Luchi. "We've missed you. Any luck talking your parents round?"

Indira shakes her head. "Nope. I've been stuck in here for a whole week! Believe me, I've missed you too."

"You up for plan B then?" asks Luchi.

Indira replies by swinging her legs out over the windowsill. "Help me, Luchi?" she asks. Her room is on the ground floor but the window is quite high up on the wall.

"You can jump from there!" Luchi scoffs.

"Are you kidding?" retorts Indira. "How would I explain a broken ankle to my parents?"

Luchi sighs and steps forward, helping her down. "You're such a drama queen! No wonder you want to be an actor so much," he teases.

"Freedom!" says Indira, ignoring the jibe. "I just hope

Mum doesn't look in on me. She gave me my mobile back at the weekend, and Sunita's going to try and warn me if she starts snooping. Let's go!"

"Your sister's on your side then?" asks Luchi, and Indira nods. "Cool."

"Did you try talking to your parents?" I ask as we run to meet Alfie.

"I talked myself blue in the face all week!"

"Why are they doing this?" I ask her. "They've always let you come to Footlights before."

"My stupid cousin failed her exams," says Indira. "And now Dad's convinced the same thing will happen to me!"

I shake my head because we're nowhere near taking exams yet. "No way," I say. "You're so smart – you couldn't fail if you *tried*!"

As we enter the theatre, some of the cast are already practising a dance routine with Lauren.

"Hi Indira!" says Badger. "I'm really glad to see you. Are you feeling better now?"

"Better?" says Indira, confused, and then she remembers the excuse we gave for her absence. "Oh… er… yes, much better thanks, Mr Beaven," she replies unconvincingly.

"Good! You've got a lot of the routine to catch up on. Why don't you just watch with me the first time through?"

We dance for an hour. Indira joins in and does really well – in fact, we all do. There's an exhilarating sense that it's all starting to come together. Even Lauren is smiling.

"Great work, kids," says Badger as we all stop for a drink, puffing and happy. "It's looking brilliant. Take a break and then, now that Indira's back, we'll rehearse that opening scene with Beauty's whole family."

"It's so good to have you back, Indira," I tell her as we sit side by side on the floor.

"It's great to *be* back," she says with a quick smile. She sounds as though she means it, but she glances at her phone. I know she's worried about getting caught.

"I've got something to tell everyone," Taylor announces. "My mum's found out there's a big council meeting at the town hall on Friday morning. I think we should march there and present the petition. It's a great opportunity."

"I thought we were going to collect signatures at the cake sale?" says Alfie with a frown. "Won't that leave us really short?"

"Yes, but this is the last meeting before their holiday," Taylor explains. "It's now or never!"

"I think we should go for it," says Badger. "I'll speak to the police, and we can all try and get some more signatures over the next few days!"

"The police?" Alice squeaks. Everyone laughs.

"You have to inform the police before you hold a demo," says Badger. "I know this is only a tiny one, but better safe than sorry."

The rehearsal goes well. Indira has learned her lines better than any of us while she was supposed to be studying. Surprisingly, Lauren is the one who doesn't know hers yet.

"Right, Lauren," Badger says as we're all packing up to go home. "You've worked really hard on the dances and they're great, but I need you to crack on and learn those lines now! OK?"

To my surprise, Lauren blushes and looks really awkward. "I will," she promises meekly.

Indira is rushing me out. "I need to get back," she urges me. "Quickly! It's nearly time for tea and I'll be caught for sure!"

We race back to Indira's house and Luchi helps her climb back into her room.

"All clear," she whispers out of the window. "See you tomorrow."

"It's crazy that she has to sneak around," I say. "Everything's going wrong this summer. Why can't it just all be fun like it usually is?"

Luchi shrugs. "I dunno. D'you want to come to my place for tea, then we can go round the flats after and get some people to sign our petition?"

"Cool," I say. "I'll just call in at home so they know where I am."

* * *

We help Indira sneak out again the next day. She looks tired. "I had to stay up late studying," she tells me. "You won't believe it, but Dad actually gave me a test this morning."

"Seriously?" I say.

"I know, he's *way* over the top," she replies, looking glum.

36

"Look, would you rather just give up Footlights?" I ask.

"No way! I'm in. Lead on!"

The rehearsal goes really well again. Badger announces it's time to start acting without our scripts. Taylor's working on Beast's costume – which looks fantastic – but she has to keep prompting Lauren who gets stuck *a lot*. In the end she gives up on the outfit and starts saying all Beauty's lines so Lauren can repeat them. We're almost at the end of a scene and Indira is speaking when a mobile rings.

"OK, who's left their mobile on?" says Badger despairingly.

"Me," says Indira looking worried. She rushes over to her bag and fumbles for her phone with shaking hands. She holds it up to her ear and the room is quiet, waiting for her. We can all hear that whoever is on the other end is shouting furiously. Indira listens a few moments, then bursts into tears and runs out of the hall without even saying goodbye.

"What's going on?" asks Badger bewildered.

Luchi and I look at each other guiltily.

"Er… her nan isn't very well," says Luchi.

Badger looks suspicious, but doesn't say any more.

We carry on as best we can with Taylor reading in Indira's part as well.

Chapter 6

Disaster Strikes

Indira doesn't turn up the next day or the day after. At the end of Thursday's rehearsal Badger calls me over. "I'd like you to explain what's going on with Indira please, Zoe," he asks. "The truth this time."

I take a deep breath. "OK. Indira's parents decided she couldn't come to Footlights any more," I tell him. "She's tried talking them round, but they won't listen."

"Was that why she went missing for a week?"

I blush. "Um… yeah."

"So explain to me what she was doing here earlier this week," he says, sounding cross.

I squirm uncomfortably. I'm really not enjoying this conversation. "Luchi and I helped her sneak out," I confess.

Badger gives me his 'disappointed' look.

"I see. And have you heard from her since?"

I shake my head. "She's not replying to texts and she didn't answer when we knocked on her window today," I tell him.

"Right, I'll deal with this at the end of rehearsal. Tell Luchi to stay behind with you, please," he says gravely.

I don't enjoy myself as much as usual after that because I'm worried about what Badger's going to say. When everyone's left, he gives us a telling off that makes my eyes water. The words 'selfish' and 'irresponsible' come up a lot.

"We're all going to Indira's now to apologize to her parents," says Mr Beaven.

"What?" cries Luchi.

"Now?" I gasp.

"Right now. I'll try and persuade Mr and Mrs Parekh to let Indira join the club again. I'm not sure I'll succeed though. You've made my job much harder," says Badger. "You should have come to me first. Do you understand?"

"Indira's parents really don't like me," says Luchi. "It might be better if I don't come–"

"You're coming!" snaps Badger. We trail after him meekly and don't argue any more.

About halfway to the flats, Badger slows down. He seems pale and out of breath. "Are you all right, Mr Beaven?" Luchi asks concerned.

He mops his face with his handkerchief. He's sweating even though it's not hot this evening.

"I'm feeling a little odd," he admits, taking a few deep breaths. "Don't worry, I'll be fine. Let's just get this over with."

Indira's father opens the door and doesn't look pleased to see us.

"Hello, Mr Parekh, I'm Mr Beaven – the drama

teacher at Footlights," Badger says. "Could we possibly come in and speak to you for a few moments?"

Mr Parekh hesitates, but then grudgingly opens the door and lets us in.

First, Badger makes us apologize. It's horrible. Indira's mum and dad just stare at us disapprovingly. "Indira's my *best* friend," I say finally.

"You are not a good friend to her!" says Mrs Parekh. "You encourage her to be disobedient and disrespectful to her parents!"

I feel hurt because I've never thought of it like that. "You're right, and I'm really sorry!" I say. "But I *am* a good friend to her. She's really talented, you know, and she loves being on the stage. It means as much to her as it does to me – that's why I helped her. We didn't mean to upset anyone. I'll help Indira to study if it means she can carry on with Footlights, too!"

Indira's mum and dad just carry on frowning at me, so Badger takes over.

"I came here tonight to offer an apology," he says, "but also to explain why it's so important to us that Indira is part of this production. She is one of our most talented young actors and I believe she, of all the students, could have a real future in film and theatre. She–"

"That's *not* the sort of future I want for *my* daughter!" interrupts Mr Parekh vehemently. "Strutting around on stage, getting paid a pittance! That's no future!"

"As a matter of fact," Badger tries again, "There's a great deal of work in teaching and related disciplines for actors–"

"Indira could be a doctor or a dentist!" This time it's Mrs Parekh who interrupts. "She needs to study hard and not waste her time with this acting nonsense!"

I can see Badger re-evaluating his arguments swiftly. He's starting to sweat again. "The performing arts are excellent for improving memory, poise, voice control, speaking and confidence," he says. "All these things will stand her in really good stead, no matter what her career choices!"

"Confidence?" cries Mr Parekh. "That girl has far too much confidence already! What she needs is discipline and proper ambition. You! You are just here because you need her for your trivial little play! You don't care about her future, any of you! Look at *you*," he shouts at Mr Beaven, his voice rising. "Teaching in a kids' drama club for pennies. Where did all your drama get you? Nowhere! Just nowhere!"

"As a matter of fact," says Mr Beaven, breathing heavily, "I'm deputy head teacher of The Firs. You may know it; it's an elite boarding school on the outskirts of the city. Many of my students go on to RADA and other top drama colleges. I run Footlights in the holidays to share my skills with… less privileged children. I don't need the money. That's not why I…." he pauses and gasps, his hand clutching his chest.

"Are you all right, Mr Beaven?" I ask, concerned. He's as white as a sheet and his eyes are glassy. "Can he have a drink of water or something, please?" I ask Mrs Parekh.

She fetches a glass at once. I'm really frightened for Badger who's looking worse and worse. At last he manages to speak. "I'm sorry I wasted your time, Mr Parekh," he says breathlessly. "I can see you're angry and you're not going to change your...." He tries to finish his sentence, but only gulps painfully. As we watch, his eyes bulge and then close, and he slides out of his chair on to the floor.

"Mr Beaven!" Luchi and I rush to him as Mrs Parekh grabs the phone to call an ambulance. I pull off my jumper and slide it under Badger's head to make him more comfortable. Luchi loosens his tie and puts a hand on his chest.

"His heart's still beating, but it's weird – out of time," he says anxiously. "I think he's having a heart attack!"

* * *

Luchi and I don't talk much on the way to the demo the following morning. My mum is with me, pushing the twins, and Luchi's brought his granddad. Alfie meets us with his mum and two younger brothers. There's a really good crowd of people when we reach the theatre. Even Lauren is there, which surprises me. Mr Beaven's nowhere to be seen, of course.

"Where's Badger?" Taylor asks me. "He promised to be here!"

"He was taken ill yesterday," I tell her. "We went round to talk to Indira's parents and he... sort of... collapsed!"

"Oh no! Is he OK?" asks Taylor. The others are all listening now too.

"We don't know," says Luchi. "They took him away in an ambulance. He was unconscious."

The others gasp and pelt us with questions. They're as worried about him as we are.

"Should we carry on with the march, or not?" asks Taylor. "It seems really wrong without Badger."

"But this is our only chance!" cries Lauren.

"And the police are outside waiting to escort us," says Alfie. "I think he'd want us to go ahead, wouldn't he?"

"Yes," I agree. "Let's go."

We all pick up the banners that Taylor, Alice and some of the others have made and go outside. I hold one side of a banner that says **"Save our drama club!"** in big red letters.

People stand and stare as we pass by – about fifty of us, all ages, walking together. It feels really good, to be doing something – standing up for ourselves. The police escort makes the protest official and serious.

When we reach the town hall we stand outside and chant "No cuts! Save our club!"

We can see the meeting going on inside. One of the councillors gets up and closes the window and the curtain too, so we chant more loudly. "NO CUTS! SAVE OUR CLUB! NO CUTS! SHAME ON YOU!"

The police look bored. It's not as if anything exciting or dangerous is going to happen. I wonder whether the councillors can even hear us now.

"We have to do something to get their attention," says Taylor, obviously thinking the same thing as me.

"What, like throw eggs at their windows?" asks Luchi.

"*Luchi*," reprimands his grandfather. "That sort of behaviour won't get you anywhere."

"Just joking, gramps," Luchi says, laughing.

"I think we should ask if we can plead our case to the councillors," says Taylor as a few of the others turn to listen.

"Huh! Who's going to do that? *You?*" asks Lauren, scowling. "They'll laugh at you."

"She's right," says Alfie. "If anyone was going to talk to the council it would have to be Mr Beaven. And he's not here."

"I'm not scared," says Taylor. "And it wouldn't be the first time I've been laughed at," she hisses, glaring at Lauren. I think back to the first rehearsal when Lauren, Bailey and Alice mocked her and I get angry all over again.

"I'll go with you," I say, almost before I realize what I'm doing.

"Really?" says Taylor. "Cool!"

"I think you'll do a great job," says Luchi, beaming at us both. "All in favour say 'Aye'."

Everyone shouts out, "AYE!"

Everyone except Lauren, that is. "Well, I think you'll embarrass yourselves," she says, flicking her hair and walking away.

Taylor and I go into the reception and ask to present our petition to the meeting.

"I can't allow that," says the woman behind the desk firmly.

"Very well then," says Taylor. "We'll keep chanting

44

outside your offices until the meeting's over."

"You'd do better to go home, dear," says the receptionist patronizingly. "This is a closed meeting, you see – members of the public aren't permitted." She turns away, pushes her glasses firmly on to her nose and answers the phone.

Taylor and I turn to leave. I've lost all my fight, and feel like a deflated balloon.

"Hey, Zoe!" Taylor whispers. "The councillors are just on the other side of that door. Why don't we just... go in?"

"What?" I reply, stunned.

"What are they going to do? Throw out a girl in a wheelchair?" She grins at me mischievously. "Are you with me?"

Chapter 7

Team Work

There are butterflies in my belly as I whisper: "Yes, let's do it."

I walk into the room, holding the door open so Taylor can follow me through. I can hear my friends still chanting outside.

The meeting is huge. I totally wasn't expecting so many faces to all turn towards me in one go. I gulp. I think I might be sick. But Taylor seems completely unfazed and wheels herself forward. "We're from Footlights – the local drama club," she says loudly. "We've come here today to beg you to reconsider your decision to withdraw our funding!"

Oh boy. I stand there awkwardly, trying my best to look as if I know what I'm doing, just like Taylor.

"How dare you burst in here?" begins a stern-looking older man in a horrible tweed suit.

Taylor smiles at him and speaks up a bit louder: "This is Zoe, who has been a member longer than anyone. She'd like to tell you what the club means to her."

Taylor grabs my hand and pulls me forward.

"Who let you in here?" demands a woman in a purple blouse and matching lipstick. "This is a closed meeting. You don't have permission to—"

"Please!" says Taylor. "Just listen to Zoe for a couple of minutes. Then I promise we'll go."

Incredibly, they all fall silent and look at me. Despite being so terrified that my voice shakes, I start to speak: "I've been in Footlights since it started three years ago," I tell them. "It's been the best thing in my whole life. Without it, the holidays would be empty. I'd have nowhere to go."

I'm warming up now. If I just pretend I'm on the stage, speaking a part, I don't feel so scared. The faces are the audience. "I live on the Markfields estate. Last week, I saw a group of kids there vandalising the new trees and shrubs you've so kindly planted." A grumble goes around the room, "It's not because they're bad, but because there's nothing for them to do. We don't want to be like that. We want to carry on learning to act, to dance and to work together. Footlights has given me the confidence to speak to you here now. I could never have done that before. There are nearly thirty of us involved in Footlights. We're just ordinary kids, but it's taught us all so much. Please don't take it away."

I stop, unsure what else I can say. I've got tears in my eyes because I care so much. The councillors stare at us in stony silence. I don't get a good feeling.

"You are all invited to our performance in two weeks time!" says Taylor brightly. "We'll send you some tickets.

It would be really great to have your support. Thank you for listening!"

She spins her chair around and heads for the door. I mumble "Thank you!" and rush to open it for her. As we leave, the receptionist puts down the phone and spots us. "I told you not to go in there!" she cries angrily. But we don't hang about to be told off, whisking ourselves out of the building.

When we emerge into the sunshine, the others stop chanting and crowd around us asking, "How did it go?" and "What did they say?"

I'm sure it went badly, but Taylor says: "It was great. They listened and Zoe spoke out brilliantly." She beams at me. "We both did our best."

* * *

Mr Jones is waiting for us when we get back to the theatre. "Have you heard anything about Mr Beaven?" I ask him anxiously. "Is he all right?"

"He's still in hospital," says Mr Jones. "But he's stable, though – out of danger. In fact, I've just spoken to him on the phone."

I sigh with relief.

"Does that mean he's going to get better?" asks Luchi. He looked pretty bad last night."

"I hope he'll be fine eventually," Mr Jones tells us. The word 'eventually' is ominous.

"What about Footlights this summer? What about *Beauty and the Beast*?" I ask. "Will we have to cancel it?"

This might be our very last show and everything is falling apart. No Indira, Lauren spoiling things and now Badger being ill. I can't see any kind of happy ending right now.

"Well, obviously Mr Beaven's very sorry not to be here at the moment," says Mr Jones. "But he said he hopes you'll all go ahead with the cake sale tomorrow."

"Cool," says Luchi. "Can we visit him… at the hospital?"

"I'm sure he'd appreciate that," says Mr Jones. "Actually, he told me he'd like to speak to you, Zoe, as soon as possible. Shall I drive you both there now?"

"He wants to talk to *me*?" I ask, at the same time as Luchi says "Can Alfie come?"

Mr Jones laughs. "Yes, and yes," he replies.

* * *

Badger is lying in a hospital bed attached to all sorts of tubes and bleeping machines. He looks terrible; really sickly and there are dark shadows like bruises under his eyes. He turns his head, sees us and smiles wanly.

"Hey kids," he says. There's a trace of his jaunty self in his voice and we all grin with relief.

"You gave us a scare, sir!" says Luchi. "I thought you were a goner!"

Alfie elbows him for being tactless, but Badger laughs weakly. "To tell the truth, so did I, Luchi," he says. "Happily, I'm still with you. I've been thinking about the play, though."

I hold my breath. Has he brought us all the way across town just to tell us it's over?

"It's going to be a few days, probably a week until I'm fit for anything. Maybe longer. I'm so sorry. I know I'm letting you all down."

That's it. He's going to call the whole thing off. Misery and disappointment flood me. It's all been for nothing. Learning the lines and the dance routines, Taylor's hard work on the costumes, Indira getting into trouble; it was all wasted. "It's not your fault, Mr Beaven," I say sadly. "You can't help getting sick. Do you want me to tell everyone that it's all cancelled?"

"No, I certainly don't! Come on, Zoe, we won't give in as easily as all that, will we? I have a special favour to ask you. Would you take over as director for a few days until I get back? I know you'd be brilliant. And you'd have Luchi and Alfie here to back you up."

"Really?" I gasp. "You'd trust me to do that?"

I'm in a daze as we drive back across town. Badger told me exactly what we should be working on over the next few days and I wrote it all down on a scrap of paper. I'm clutching it in my hand right now. I can hardly believe it. Badger didn't give me the lead role this summer, but he trusts me (*me!*) to direct the rehearsals. Wow!

"Don't forget I'll be there to keep an eye on things," says Mr Jones as he drops us off at the flats. "You aren't on your own."

"Thanks, Mr Jones!" says Alfie politely. "And thanks for the lift."

"I can't believe this," I say to Luchi as we watch Mr Jones' car disappear.

"Badger trusts you, Zo'," says Luchi, slinging an arm around me. "You'll be fine. And we'll help, won't we Alfie?" I glow with happiness.

"'Course," says Alfie. "See you for the cake sale tomorrow. My mum had cake tins, eggs and icing stuff all over the kitchen this morning. Hopefully there'll be some leftovers that need eating up!"

"Hey, I'll go with you," says Luchi, abandoning me for the prospect of cake. Huh!

"I'm baking too," I shout, but they obviously have more faith in Alfie's mum's skills than mine, because they're halfway down the road already.

Chapter 8

Cakes and Confrontations

My chocolate fudge cake turns out pretty well. I've also made a tin full of rocky road to sell with the coffees. Mum flipped out when she saw the kitchen. She said it looked as if a chocolate bomb had gone off. I laughed, which totally didn't help the situation.

I get to the hall early with Luchi (who persuaded his granddad to help him bake his delicious West Indian bun). There's a crowd in the entrance hall.

"So what's going on?" asks Luchi. They stand back and the full horror hits us. Someone, no prizes for guessing who, has made a big poster for the show. But it's not the one we agreed on. It says **Beauty and the Beast** across the top all right, but underneath it says 'Starring Lauren Rivers – as seen on *Casualty*' and there's a big, glamorous picture of Goldie. It reminds me of the pantomime posters I've seen featuring famous soap stars.

"What the…?" I exclaim.

"Yeah, right," says Taylor disgustedly. "How *dare* she?

This is everyone's show. We're all working hard, even if we aren't playing Beauty."

"Too right," I agree, thinking of the fabulous costumes Taylor is making.

Then Alfie arrives with his mum and we forget all about Lauren.

"Look at that!" I practically shriek. And everyone turns. Alfie's mum is carrying the most amazing cake. It's a huge creamy butterfly with wings studded with a shower of sparkling sweets.

"That's way too awesome to just sell!" exclaims Taylor. "We should raffle it!"

"I'll get some tickets from the stationer's," offers Bailey.

* * *

The cake sale is manic. It feels as if every resident in a ten-mile radius has turned up to buy home-made cake, so Alice's leaflets worked a treat.

The cakes completely sell out and I make what feels like a billion teas and coffees. I'm just cutting up the last of the cakes we've put aside to serve when I look up and there's Indira – right in front of me – with both her parents. She's smiling.

"Indira!" I cry, edging out from behind the table to give her a hug. "You came!" I'm so pleased to see her, I can't stop grinning like a maniac. Mr and Mrs Parekh buy tea and cake while Indira tells me she's got some good news.

"I'm allowed to come back!" she says. "Dad was so shocked by poor Badger getting ill like that. It made him feel *well* guilty. We had a long talk and, basically, he's agreed that I should be allowed some time off in the holidays. I can come to Footlights and be in the play as long as I study every morning."

"That's soooo great," I say. "It's no fun without you!" Then I go to Mr and Mrs Parekh and thank them for letting Indira come back.

I don't even get a piece of cake in the end – we sell every last crumb. Alfie claims he made two thousand and three jugs of squash. He's so chuffed that *everyone* bought raffle tickets for his mum's cake.

"We've made nearly three hundred pounds!" I say, stunned, once everybody has finally gone and we've cleaned up and counted the money. "We can get everything you need for the costumes now, Taylor! *And* there'll be money left over!"

Luchi stretches and yawns. "Man, that was hard work," he says. "I need to go home and chill."

"Me too," agrees Alfie. "I'm glad mum's cake went to that family in the end. The kids were practically drooling when they won it."

"It was brilliant," I say. "I bet that cake raised as much as everything else put together."

"It pretty much did," agreed Taylor. "I notice Lauren didn't bother to turn up today, despite being the *star* of the show."

"It was embarrassing!" says Luchi. "I was selling tickets at the door with Bailey and everyone kept looking at the poster and asking where she was. Bailey says Lauren's dad got the posters made."

"Well, she *has* got the most lines to learn and the dances to choreograph," says Alfie.

"True about the dances," I say. "But I haven't noticed that she's learned her lines yet."

"Ease up on her, Zo'," says Alfie mildly. It annoys me that he always sticks up for her.

"She's asking for it, putting herself on the posters like that!" I say indignantly.

* * *

Monday's rehearsal goes well. At first I'm nervous about being in charge, but I gradually get used to it. Taylor stands in for me on stage so that I can watch everyone else. It feels really different, but I have several ideas on how to improve things. Lauren mutters a bit when I give her direction, but everyone does what I say.

"Great work, everyone!" I call out at the end. "See you tomorrow."

"Who does she think she is?" I hear Lauren say to Bailey. I ignore her. It's gone well today.

* * *

Ideas for the play run around my head all night, like dogs chasing cats. Short on sleep, I'm not in a great mood the next day when Lauren starts mouthing off at me for being rubbish at dancing. "You're useless, Zoe," she taunts me, just because I get a couple of little things wrong. "You're going to spoil my whole show!"

"It's not *your* show!" I say angrily. "It's ours – all of us!"

"I'm the star. It's my name on the posters!"

"Yeah, because *you* put it there!" I snap.

"Chill, ladies," says Luchi. "Can we get on with the dance?"

* * *

By Friday, I've mastered the dance steps, but Lauren *still* doesn't know her lines. We're rehearsing the scene near the end where she's come back to Beast because he's ill. Luchi's lying on the stage and Lauren keeps putting her hands on his arms and chest – it's annoying the life out of me. When she stops for about the fifth time and looks at Taylor for her line, I lose my patience.

"Lauren, our performance is in *one week*! How can you *still* not know your words?" I demand. "Honestly, the only line you've learned so far is 'Beast, I love you!' – and that's only 'cos you fancy Luchi!"

Lauren springs to her feet, colour flaming in her cheeks. "I didn't come here to be ordered about by some loser who knows less about performing than I do!" she shouts.

"Hey, Lauren…." Luchi starts to say, but both Lauren and I are too furious to listen. Indira puts a hand on my arm to try and calm me down, but I shake her off.

"We don't want you here at all!" I shout at Lauren.

"Flicking your hair extensions about and thinking you're better than the rest of us. We did a lot better before you came along!"

"Fine!" says Lauren, marching off the stage and picking up her bag. "Do without me! See how rubbish your show will be then!" She storms out of the hall, banging the door behind her.

"Great," says Luchi sitting up and looking at me reproachfully. "What are we going to do now? We need her and you know it."

"She's worked so hard on the dances," Alice pipes up. "They're the best we've ever had."

"But she's impossible!" I cry. Anger is still boiling and bubbling inside me.

"We know," says Indira calmly. "But you were perhaps a bit out of order there too, Zo'. Badger wouldn't have lost his temper like that."

"Maybe not, but any of us could play Beauty!" I argue. "We don't need her."

"We do," says Alfie, emerging from his sound studio at the back. "She's perfect for Beauty and there's still time for her to learn the lines. Maybe she just needs some… help?"

I'm about to have a go at Alfie for sticking up for Lauren yet again, but I bite my tongue. Falling out with my friends isn't going to help anything.

Chapter 9

Rows and Revelations

Everyone's looking at me, expecting me to sort this out. I stand up and take a deep breath. What would Badger do now? The truth is, I have no idea.

"OK, I've made my decision," I say as confidently as I can. "Indira, I need you to take on the role of Beauty... and Alice, you can play the mother instead of Indira.... I think we should finish for today and work extra hard tomorrow to make up. Thanks, everyone!"

My voice sounds a bit shaky, but I think that was pretty convincing. Wasn't it? Maybe not, since, instead of packing up, they're all still standing staring at me.

"You're not serious?" says Indira at last.

"I am," I say firmly. "It's by far the best option." Then I lower my voice and speak for Indira's ears only. "Be my mate and just do it?" I beg her.

"What's all this?" says Mr Jones, wandering in from the little kitchen with a mug of tea in his hand. "Are you finishing already?"

"Yes, we've done enough for today," I tell him. The

others start leaving, shaking their heads. Indira grabs my arm and marches me outside.

"Zoe, what are you thinking?" she demands. "Do you *seriously* expect me to learn all of Beauty's lines in a week? And all her dances too? Have you forgotten I have to study every day?"

"No, I haven't," I assure her. "Sorry Indira, I just panicked. But you can do it, I know you can. Badger told your parents you were the most talented student of us all. He said you had a future on the stage! He should have given *you* the role in the first place!"

"He said that? Really?" Indira bites her lip. I can tell from the dreamy look in her eyes that she can totally see herself as Beauty. She's tempted. "OK, look I'll talk to my parents–"

"Thanks!" I blurt out, hugging her.

"But I'm not promising anything," she adds, giggling.

Luchi walks home with us but he's grouchy. "What was I supposed to do?" I try to ask him. "Lauren was the one who stormed out!"

"Whatever, Zoe," he says, peeling off and heading home.

* * *

The rehearsal the next day is awful. Indira doesn't know her lines and nor does Alice who has reluctantly agreed to play the mother. "I'm only doing this to help out," she says, glaring at me. "I don't even *want* this part."

It doesn't take long before Indira gets stuck during the dance with Beast. Luchi tries to help, but he has only a hazy idea of Beauty's steps.

"Zoe, Lauren choreographed these dances," says Indira at last, giving up and sitting down. "Nobody else knows Beauty's steps! And I can't even do half the stuff she could do, like the splits."

"You don't need to," I say. "Put in steps you can do."

Indira shakes her head. "I can't just make stuff up," she says grumpily. "I've got enough to do."

"Look, we'll worry about the dancing tomorrow," I say decisively. "Let's work on the lines first!"

We read through the scene a couple of times and, by the end, Indira already knows them better than Lauren did. She and Luchi work really well together and Indira looks great on the stage. She has the same poise and confidence as Lauren, without the arrogance.

Quite a few of the others clearly aren't happy though, including Alice. "I can't DO this!" she says after Taylor prompts her for the tenth time. "How does anyone learn all these lines? I'm not surprised Lauren was struggling. Are you going to throw *me* out now *too*?" she asks, giving me another resentful look.

"Give me a break, guys!" I beg them, starting to get really stressed.

"Like you gave *Lauren* a break, you mean?" mutters Bailey.

We all hear her. I look around wondering if everyone else agrees – even my friends. None of them is exactly on my side any more.

In the break, I get a text from Badger: "How's it going, Zoe?"

I reply: "OK. Sort of. R u better?"

It's not true of course – things aren't going even 'sort of' OK. We've got three days until the show and it's a total disaster zone.

"Much better thanx. Back b4 show, I hope," Badger texts back.

He *hopes*! What does that mean? I was hoping he'd be back… today. I was hoping he'd walk through the door right–

"Are you freaking out, Zoe?" Taylor asks, bringing her wheelchair to a halt beside me.

"Um… yeah, does it show?"

Taylor grins. "It'll be alright on the night, you know," she tells me.

"Says who?" I ask bitterly.

"It's an old theatre saying, I think… or maybe a TV show. Anyway, I'll tell you something else. I googled 'what makes a great theatre director' last night."

"Oh yes?" I say. "Did it say 'no one by the name of Zoe, ever'?"

"It's a lot of responsibility," Taylor says kindly. "Lauren wasn't making things easy. But the job is about working with the cast – encouraging them. A good director will be professional and supportive at all times."

"Right. That's me out, then."

"You can do it, Zoe," she says. "I believe in you."

* * *

After the rehearsal, I notice Alfie, Indira and Luchi leaving without me. Feeling rejected, I finish clearing up by myself and then slump into one of the chairs. I'm completely miserable. How could I ever have thought being asked to direct was a good thing? I haven't even had a chance to learn my own part properly, I've been so busy concentrating on everyone else's.

I can't help it, tears start dripping down my cheeks. Right at that moment, the door opens unexpectedly. I look up, horrified to be caught crying, wiping my face dry with my sleeve.

I'm astonished to see Lauren walk in. She pulls up a chair and sits down opposite me. She's twisting her hair around her fingers and giving me sideways glances. She takes a deep breath and says, "I'm sorry I walked out."

I stare and see Lauren's been crying too. Her face is all blotchy and her eyelids are swollen. It never occurred to me she would get so upset.

"I'm… I'm sorry too," I say. "About the things I said. I was out of order."

"Yeah, I know," Lauren smirks, a bit like her old self. "My hair's totally natural," she tells me, performing her trademark flick. "Not extensions."

I smile just the tiniest bit. "I know," I admit.

"Luchi said I should come and talk to you."

She's been talking to Luchi? Argh. The heat of jealousy and frustration rise up inside me. But then I think of Taylor's advice – a good director will be professional and supportive at all times.

I take a minute to compose myself, and look Lauren

straight in the eye. "Look, I was wrong, we need you–"

"Great," says Lauren with a sigh. "That's sorted then. I'm really looking forward to being Beauty."

"Ah," I say, trying to keep my voice calm and friendly. "The thing is, Lauren... I've given that role to Indira now."

"WHAT?" Lauren practically screams. "To *Indira*? But it's *my* part!"

"Lauren, you did walk out. For two days! And, you aren't the, um, easiest person to work with, you know."

Luchi saunters in. I suspect he's been listening the whole time.

"Zoe's right, Lauren," he says. "Yes, she was unfair and said stuff she shouldn't. But you never let up on her either... and you *didn't* learn your lines." He looks at me, then at Lauren, as if he's weighing up what to say next. Then he shrugs. "Indira will make a good Beauty – if you'll help her with the dancing, Lauren."

"You want me to teach Indira *my* dance steps... and you don't want me in the play at all?" says Lauren, in a small and very un-Lauren-like voice. She sniffs and wipes away a tear. Suddenly I feel really, really bad.

"You could play the mother," I offer. "Alice really doesn't want to do it. She hates having a speaking part. But you'd have to learn the lines. Properly."

"Yeah, about that," says Lauren, blushing. "The thing is...." she huffs, hesitating, and I wonder what on earth she's about to say. "I'm... well... I'm, like, *really* dyslexic."

"What? But you played Annie before!" I point out.

"Yeah, but I learned the lines off the DVD," she explains, her cheeks burning. "I just listened to them over and over again. There isn't a DVD of this script, though... so I've been stuck."

"Why didn't you tell us?" demands Luchi.

"Because it's embarrassing, of course. Duh!" Lauren replies, rolling her eyes again. "How would you like people knowing you can barely read?" she asks.

"I would have helped you learn the lines!" says Luchi.

I feel a lump of jealousy in my throat again, but I swallow it down. It's the play that matters and, at the moment, I'm still in charge.

"We'd all have helped you if we'd known! I'm sorry Lauren... again. Look can we compromise here, please? Will you play the part of mother and help Indira with Beauty?" I ask. "And Luchi can, um, help you learn your lines. Right, Luchi?"

Lauren grimaces, muttering that it's humiliating. I think of the posters and I can see how she feels, but I'm not about to let Indira down after everything.

"OK," sighs Lauren at last.

"Thank you," I say, smiling at her.

And just like that, everything is settled. I feel as if I could pass out with relief.

When we reach the flats, Luchi grabs me in a big bear hug. "You did a good thing today, Zo'," he says. "I'm proud of you."

"Um... thanks," I call awkwardly as he walks away.

Chapter 10

The Final Curtain

We work *so hard* over the next three days, practising from morning till night. Badger doesn't show up, but it's all right, because there's no more fighting. We're heads-down, focused and one hundred per cent dedicated.

Lauren swans around, confident as ever, but unusually nice at the same time. "Great costumes, Taylor," she says at the dress rehearsal.

"Yeah, you're so talented," Alice adds and Taylor beams. It feels as if we're all part of a team at last.

Luchi looks awesome in his Beast costume. He's a hideous monster. Indira has no trouble looking terrified of him on stage. "Am I ugly?" he growls at Beauty, towering over her. "Frightened?" he roars, thrusting his masked face into Indira's.

"Yes, Beast!" she says recoiling in horror.

"Tone it down a bit, Luchi?" I suggest. "We don't want Beauty fainting on stage!"

* * *

We rehearse the entire day on Saturday. Indira is amazing at learning lines and knows them all perfectly. Lauren is not bad either now that Luchi has helped her. Beauty's mother is clearly a better dancer than Beauty herself. Lauren knows it, but for once she doesn't boast.

Two hours before the performance, Badger shows up. "Mr Beaven!" we all yell, crowding round him.

"Great to see you," he says, laughing. "But let me get some air!"

We all back off and give him a seat at the front. "I hope I've arrived in time for the final run-through?" he asks once he's comfortable and Mr Jones has fetched him a coffee.

I see Mr Jones wink at him. They're friends and I suddenly wonder whether he's been telling Badger far more about what's really been going on than I have. Badger calls me over to sit next to him.

"So, Zoe," he says. "It seems you've changed some of the roles about a bit. What happened?" His voice is a little stern.

I hesitate. Then I tell him the truth. "Lauren and I had a big fight," I admit.

"I see. And whose fault do you feel that was?"

"Well, she…." I begin. Then I stop. "It was my fault," I say. "I lost my temper. I forgot a director needs to be professional."

"It was my fault too," says Lauren, walking on to the stage in front of us. "I was being mean to Zoe. And then I walked out and left them all in the lurch."

"Indira stepped in," adds Taylor. "To save the play."

Badger looks from one to the other of us. "Well," he says. "As long as you've worked through it and sorted it out, that's what's important." He smiles at us. I'm *so* relieved.

* * *

By seven o'clock, the theatre is almost overflowing. Every seat is taken, and people are standing at the back. All our friends and relations are here, and some teachers from school, too. Mr Beaven is sitting in the front row with his wife on one side of him and an older woman on the other. I've never seen her before, but I wonder whether it might be his mother.

Backstage, Alice and Bailey are fixing everyone's make-up and Lauren and Indira are practising some steps together. The nerves are really getting to us all now. There are knots in my belly, my hands are shaking and I feel sick.

Lauren starts the show. Everyone catches their breath when she dances on to the stage in a pale blue dress, picked out by one of Alfie's spotlights. "Long ago, in a city far away, there lived a merchant!" she begins.

It all feels like a dream. At first we are a bit stiff and wooden and it's hard to really speak out to such a big audience. Gradually I get that flying feeling. I'm stepping on air and the words are flowing. I forget the audience. I forget I'm acting. There's just the story and the dance steps, like a river flowing steadily between its banks.

There are a few rocks and rapids here and there of course: Lauren forgets her lines once and Taylor has to whisper from the wings. At one point Lauren skips a section completely, but everyone sticks with her. Indira forgets some of her dance moves, but she speaks her lines so movingly that no one really notices. She looks perfect for the part – her beautiful black hair glows and the glitter Bailey put on her skin sparkles under the lights.

Luchi pretty much steals the show. We've all been fighting over playing Beauty, but it's Beast that roars on to the stage, getting the audience clapping and stamping. He's amazing. Taylor's Beast costume is fabulous and Alfie has set up lurid green lighting, spooky sound effects and stage smoke for him.

When Luchi turns back into the prince at the end, and he and Indira kiss, the audience sigh.

Before I know what's happened, it's over and we're bowing. I spot my mum cheering, and suddenly feel very emotional. The twins are jumping up and down, waving at me, too. Then I look across to Indira's family – her parents, grandmother, brother and sister are all smiling and look really proud. Everyone's clapping and stamping their feet. They shout and whistle and give us three curtain calls before they let us go. We're all buzzing with excitement and happiness.

"We did it!" says Luchi, beaming, as we all pour into the changing room behind the stage.

"You were wonderful, Luchi," says Lauren, walking up to him. "You were the real star."

"Thanks," says Luchi turning towards me. "But actually I think it was–"

"ZOE!" Alfie appears in the doorway. "Badger wants you!"

I walk out into the theatre which is now half empty. The lights are up and the magic has gone. Two councillors are waiting for us. They came!

"We wanted to say thank you for the tickets," says the purple-lipstick woman. "We enjoyed the show very much."

"We also wanted to tell you that your appeal at the meeting really moved us," says the tweed-jacket man.

"Oh!" I exclaim, feeling really proud of myself. "Does that mean you *will* fund us after all?"

They both shake their heads. "We're sorry, but it's out of our hands," they tell me. "Our budget has been cut by the government. We have no money. If we could help you, we would. We just wanted you to know that."

I'm devastated. As they leave, I turn to Badger who has been talking to the stranger beside him. "That's it!" I say forlornly. "They aren't going to give us a penny. Footlights is over."

Indira and Luchi are beside me now and Indira takes my hand, squeezing it. "They've got no money?" she says angrily. "I bet they're still getting a fat salary, though."

"They don't care about kids like us," says Luchi. He gives the floor a small kick in frustration.

"Fortunately someone else does," says Badger, grinning. How can he be smiling? Our whole future has just crumbled to dust.

"I had a great deal of time on my hands in hospital,"

Badger explains. "I did some research on the Internet. Allow me to introduce you to Mrs Collins of the Jonathan Smith Foundation," Badger turns to the woman who was sitting beside him during the play. "Mrs Collins gives arts grants to local projects which serve the community."

We're all holding our breath now. The whole cast has come out into the almost-empty theatre and we stand motionless, hardly daring to hope, dying to hear what she has to say.

"I was *so* impressed with your show tonight!" says Mrs Collins. "How talented you all are! I'm authorized to tell you that the foundation is able to offer you a small grant to keep Footlights running for the next year at least."

If she says anything else, we don't hear it. Her voice is drowned out by all the shouting and whooping. Everyone is jumping up and down with joy and excitement.

Lauren has reached out to hug Taylor. She raises her eyebrows at me over Lauren's shoulder, which makes us both giggle.

"Thank you," I say, shaking Mrs Collins' hand. "Footlights means *so much* to us."

"So I can see," she replies, smiling kindly at us all.

"And thank *you*, Mr Beaven," I add. "Next year I'll definitely leave all the directing to you!"

He grins as I turn to celebrate with my friends.

"It's only a year," says Indira cautiously as I hug her. Alfie pats us both on the back and grins broadly.

"A whole year though!" I reply. "So much can happen in a year! Just imagine if tonight had been the last time ever!"

"Ugh, unthinkable," says Luchi, hugging us both.

I won't think too far ahead. Right now, my friends and I have Footlights and we have each other. And really, we can't ask more than that, can we?

THE END

FICTI●N EXPRESS

THE READERS TAKE CONTROL!

Have you ever wanted to change the course of a plot, change a character's destiny, tell an author what to write next?

Well, now you can!

'Drama Club' was originally written for the award-winning interactive e-book website Fiction Express.

Fiction Express e-books are published in gripping weekly episodes. At the end of each episode, readers are given voting options to decide where the plot goes next. They vote online and the winning vote is then conveyed to the author who writes the next episode, in real time, according to the readers' most popular choice.

www.fictionexpress.co.uk

WINNER
Education Resources
Award for Innovation

FICTI😮N EXPRESS

TALK TO THE AUTHORS

The Fiction Express website features a blog where readers can interact with the authors while they are writing. An exciting and unique opportunity!

FANTASTIC TEACHER RESOURCES

Each weekly Fiction Express episode comes with a PDF of teacher resources packed with ideas to extend the text.

"The teaching resources are fab and easily fill a whole week of literacy lessons!"
Rachel Humphries, teacher at Westacre Middle School

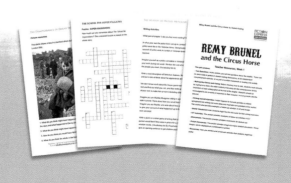

Chapter 1

Welcome to St Luthor's

Mandrake DeVille sat in the back seat of her parents'
armoured limo as it wound up the mountainside. A
sheer drop fell away to the car's left. To the right rose a
mossy cliff-face.

The bulletproof window reflected her face back to her:
black eyebrows, naturally slanted into a scowl, a small,
mean mouth, and a long, pointy nose. Her black hair
hung over one eye in a sinister curtain.

It was an evil face. Mandrake wound down her
window so she didn't have to look at it.

Far below lay a valley of dark trees, and she caught the
faint scent of pine. On top of a distant mountain peak,
she could see an ancient castle, with turrets and high,
black stone battlements.

A loud BLIP BLEEP came from the car's GPS.
Mandrake leaned forwards. "What's that?" she asked the
chauffeur, sharply. "Are we close to St Luthor's?"

St Luthor's School for Supervillains was Mandrake's
new school. She was looking forward to her first term

there about as much as a mouse looks forward to being ripped into mincemeat by a cat.

"I'm not sure what's going on," said the chauffeur, peering closer at the screen. He yanked on the steering wheel, but it didn't move. A note of panic entered his voice. "It's... I think someone's taken control of the car!"

What? Mandrake wondered. *My parents have excellent security. How could someone hack–?*

But then she stopped wondering.

She was too busy screaming.

The car was speeding off the edge of a cliff towards the wooded valley floor far, far below.

* * *

Mandrake knew in one part of her brain that they were plummeting downwards but time seemed to pause, hanging in the moment they soared off the cliff. Images flashed behind her eyes.

Then, a memory of her mother earlier that morning. Duessa DeVille was dressed for work in her Doctor Death costume, with its skull mask, long black cloak and spike-heeled boots.

"Just remember," she had said, as Mandrake climbed into the limo. "I checked your DNA carefully before growing you in the lab. One day, you could be as great a villain as I am. Who knows, maybe your telekinetic powers might even rival my own.

"Which means," her mother had continued, pointing a finger cruelly, "any failure will be entirely *your* own fault.

So, do NOT let me down. Stay strong and, more importantly, stay alive. I'd be shamed in front of my fellow villains if any child of mine showed weakness. And if you were to die… well, I'd be utterly humiliated."

Mandrake had nodded and rolled her eyes. She'd heard this all before. She knew her mother didn't actually love her enough to care if she died. And her father, Torquemada, hadn't even bothered to say goodbye. Not surprising, given that his favourite catchphrase was '*Supervillainy begins at home*'. And what's more villainous than neglecting your daughter?

Or, as both her parents preferred to call her, their 'spawn'.

Right now, Torquemada DeVille – a.k.a. Stormfront – was off threatening some Pacific island or other with extinction if its government didn't hand over their royal jewels. He wasn't bluffing. His power over storms, typhoons and other dangerous types of weather was legendary. He could easily unleash a tidal wave huge enough to flood a small country, as long as most of it wasn't too far above sea level.

Her parents expected her to become just like them. Evil. A supervillain. A master criminal. An enemy to superheroes everywhere.

But, in spite of all their efforts, she was *nothing* like them.

I'm not evil, Mandrake thought. It was a truth she barely dared to acknowledge at home, in case her parents' psychic security minions were close enough to read her thoughts.

But now, falling to almost certain death, she thought it loud and unafraid: *I don't want to be a supervillain! I want to be a superhero! I want to save the world from people… like my parents. But I'll never* be *anything unless I pull it together.*

Mandrake's mind suddenly cleared. She felt incredibly alert. More awake than she had in years.

Pull yourself together. Or you'll be a smear on the valley floor.

Mandrake closed her eyes and focused, just the way her powers tutor had taught her. She reached deep inside, allowing her power to come to the surface.

If she could just slow the car down, even a little, perhaps she could survive this?

She heard the wind rushing past the window, the chauffeur's desperate howl. It was no good. She couldn't keep her focus. She wasn't trained, not properly. She was barely able to lift an orange, never mind stop a two-tonne car in mid-air.

I'm going to die.

She watched as the ground rushed to meet her. Perhaps the car would explode? *At least it'll be a dramatic exit.*

* * *

Except, all of a sudden, the car was no longer falling. In fact, there was no longer a car.

Mandrake was standing on solid ground, in the dark. Her skin tingled, as though she'd had a mild electric shock. She felt utterly lost. It was so dark that little specks of light danced in front of her eyeballs like fireflies.

Where am I? What happened?

Mandrake held out her hands, meeting nothing at first, then her fingers brushed against skin. She flinched, and the skin's owner gasped.

The skin felt cold and unnaturally smooth to the touch. *Who has skin like that? Or what?*

Suddenly the lights came on. She was in a large, ancient hall with wood panels and a high, vaulted ceiling.

I'm inside St Luthor's. They must have teleported us. Skin-tingling was one of the side effects of teleportation. She knew this from years of family holidays. Mostly to warzones and the sites of horrific disasters... many of which her parents had caused.

She looked around.

Is this the castle I saw in the distance?

There was a group of about thirty teenagers with her in the hall. All of them seemed as scared and confused as she felt. They were mostly superhumans, but there was the odd alien too – including one *very* odd alien. He was green-skinned with eyes on stalks, standing close beside her. She realized it must have been him she'd touched in the dark, and looked away in embarrassment.

She turned her gaze to the long table at one end of the hall, where a row of terrifying figures sat looking at them with disdain.

Those must be the teachers.

The staff at St Luthor's were all retired supervillains. They wore robes, in many rich patterns and a rainbow of villainous shades, from gold and green to black and red. Their faces were the stuff of nightmares. Some were scarred, some simply monstrous, others were stunningly beautiful but so cruel you could barely look at them. Every one of them had a glint of pure, true, unmistakable evil in their eyes.

Suddenly the old man at the centre of the table rose to his feet. He wore green robes with a high, sharp collar. His eyes were green, too. He had probably been handsome, once upon a time. But now he must be ninety years old. A scar slashed his wrinkled face into two distinct parts.

"Welcome," he said, in a low, silky voice. He slid his hands behind his back and linked them there. His eyes flicked to Mandrake for a moment, and his scar-split lips curled into a smile. It was horrible. Then his gaze flicked away. "I am the headmaster of this academy. You may call me," the smile widened and grew crueller. "Master."

Mandrake wished he'd stop smiling.

"Let me offer you many insincere and meaningless apologies for the *appalling* fright you all must have had," the Master continued. His green eyes peered out from a map of wrinkles, searching his audience. "Security, you know. We couldn't possibly reveal the secret location of our facility to your lowly chauffeurs and let them live! So, we sent each of your cars off the road and teleported you out."

A gasp hissed around the room.

"Yes, I know," continued the Master. "Shame about all those lovely cars, but you've got to break a few eggs to make a wickedly delicious omelette, eh?" He gestured with his hand, waving away the multiple murders he'd just committed as though they were a slight inconvenience.

All our drivers are dead, Mandrake thought. *He's just killed... what... thirty people? And all he cares about are the cars!* Her stomach dropped as the thought sunk in. It was as though she was falling all over again. Mandrake struggled to keep her face blank, like a mask.

Don't let him know you're shocked. Don't let anyone know that you want to scream. Villains don't scream at the thought of brutal murder. They laugh with evil glee. And everyone here has to believe I'm a villain if I'm going to get out alive.

If you would like to order this book, visit the ReadZone website: www.readzonebooks.com

FICTI●N EXPRESS

The School for Supervillains
by Louie Stowell

Mandrake DeVille is heading to St Luthor's School for Supervillains, where a single act of kindness lands you in the detention pit, and only lying, cheating bullies get top marks. On paper, Mandrake's a model student: her parents are billionaire supervillains, and she has superpowers. The trouble is, Mandrake secretly wants to save the world, not destroy it.

ISBN 978-1-783-22460-9

FICTI●N EXPRESS

The Time Detectives:
The Mystery of Maddie Musgrove
by Alex Woolf

When Joe Smallwood goes to stay with his Uncle Theo and cousin Maya life seems dull, until he finds a strange smartphone nestling beside a gravestone. The phone enables Joe and Maya to become time-travelling detectives and takes them on an exciting adventure back to Victorian times. Can they prove maidservant Maddie Musgrove's innocence? Can they save her from the gallows?

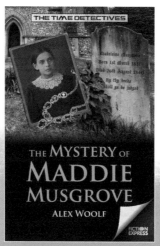

ISBN 978-1-783-22459-3

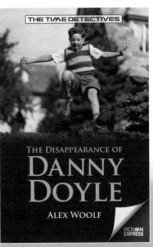

About the Author

Marie-Louise Jensen was born in Oxfordshire and has an English father and Danish mother. Her early years were largely devoted to the reading of as many books as possible, but also plagued by teachers who wanted her to spend time on less useful things (such as long division).

Marie-Louise studied Danish and German at university and has lived and worked in Denmark and Germany as well as England. She stopped full-time work to home-educate her two sons.

Since 2008 Marie-Louise has had six teen books published by Oxford University Press. She lives in Bath with her two sons and as well as reading and writing teen books and visiting schools, she also enjoys walking, swimming, going to the cinema and travelling.